For Lewis – A.C.H.

For Michael, with love – A.P.

ORCHARD BOOKS
338 Euston Road,
London NW1 3BH
Orchard Books Australia
Level 17/207 Kent Street, Sydney, NSW 2000

First published in 2014 by Orchard Books

ISBN 978 1 40832 514 8

Text © Algy Craig Hall 2014
Illustrations © Ali Pye 2014

A CIP catalogue record for this book is available from the British Library.

1 3 5 7 9 10 8 6 4 2

Printed in China

Orchard Books is a division of Hachette Children's Books,
an Hachette UK company.
www.hachette.co.uk

THE DEEP DARK WOOD

Algy Craig Hall & Ali Pye

ORCHARD

This is the **deep dark wood.**

There are lots of fierce and beastly creatures in the **deep dark wood** . . .

witches . . .

trolls . . .

giants ...

and ...

...the **big bad** wolf.

Look! Here comes a **sweet little girl**.
What is she doing in the **deep dark wood**?

Doesn't she know it's **DANGEROUS** here?

Oh, no!
The **big** bad wolf
has seen her.
This doesn't
look good.

"Hello," says the **big bad** wolf.
"Where are you going, you tasty . . .
I mean, sweet little girl?"

"I'm going to my best
friend's house for tea,"
says the little girl.

"You and your best friend are going to be MY tea," thinks the **big bad** wolf, licking his chops.

"Why don't I come with you to keep you safe?" says the naughty wolf. "A **deep dark wood** is no place for a sweet little girl, all on her own."

"Oh, thank you, Mr Wolf," says the little girl.

And together they set off, deeper into the **deep dark wood.**

"YIKES!" cries the little girl.
"Here's a witch coming to do horrible spells on us."

But the **big bad wolf** isn't even a little bit scared.

He **bristles**

and **grizzles**

and he
scares that
witch away.

"Oh, thank you, Mr Wolf,"
says the little girl, and they
walk on, deeper into the
deep dark wood.

Before long, the little girl cries out again. "HELP! There's a smelly old troll and he's coming to get us!"

The **big bad** wolf is a
tiny bit scared this time.

But he bristles

and grizzles

and claws

and
gnaws
and he
scares that
troll away.

"You're very brave, Mr Wolf," says the sweet little girl,
and they walk on, deeper into the deep dark wood.

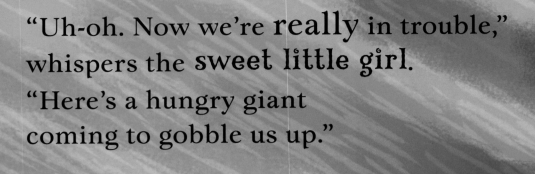

"Uh-oh. Now we're really in trouble," whispers the sweet little girl.
"Here's a hungry giant coming to gobble us up."

The **big bad wolf** really is scared this time.

But he bristles
and grizzles and claws
and gnaws
and growls
and howls

and WOW!
The **big bad wolf** manages
to scare that hungry giant away.

"Thank you very much for looking after me, Mr Wolf," says the **sweet little girl**. "Look, you've got us all the way to my best friend's house, safe and sound."

"I can't wait to eat . . . I mean **meet** her," chuckles the **big bad wolf**.

"But this is a funny place
for a little girl to live,"
says the wolf.

"Who said my best friend
was a little girl?"
says the sweet little girl.
"My best friend is . . .

...a big, scary

mon**ster.**"

"Would you like a
slice of cake?" says the
sweet little girl.

But the wolf can't hear her.

He's running away as fast as he can,
back into the **deep dark wood.**

Well, she is a **Very** scary monster . . .

. . . but she's a **lovely best friend.**